The First
100

A COLLECTION OF ONE HUNDRED WORD STORIES

ERICA L. DRAYTON

The First
100

ERICA L. DRAYTON

dedication

To my wife. She never misses an opportunity to let me know which story she likes and doesn't like.

introduction

If you ever questioned my devotion (and some might say obsessive compulsive desire) to write 100 word stories, know that almost every page, including the copyright, introduction, acknowledgments, and blurb on the back are each 100 words exactly.

I can't tell you how or why the bug bit me to give so much of my daily life to the habit of writing in bursts of 100 words at a time but these days I just can't help myself.

This is the first, but certainly not the last, of a series of books collecting my journey with writing 100 word stories.

"A question that sometimes drives me hazy: am I or the others crazy?"

— Albert Einstein

The First

100

Mahjong

#001

This was it. This was the moment I had been waiting for my whole life. Countless hours spent watching mother play with all her girlfriends and now it was my turn. I would make her proud.

My finger twitched, as it always did whenever I was about to make a mistake. Maybe I was wrong. Maybe this wasn't my time. I could feel mother's eyes rolling waiting for me to complete my turn.

I could hear the other women, my mother's dearest and ruthless friends, snigger to each other. Knowing they've won.

Then I slammed my tile on the table.

The House

#002

The morning light crept through an open window like an uninvited guest waiting to be greeted. But the house slept on.

By the afternoon, when the sun shifted like sand beneath the feet of a child running towards their mother, not a sound could be heard from within.

Finally, the sun shied away for the night. Wind waved goodbye to the curtains, and stillness fell.

Suddenly, the moon shone forth from behind dark clouds. The house creaked. Doors opened. Lights turned on. Laughter filled the air.

It's the hour of madness and mayhem.

Time to wake and scare the night.

Party

#003

Arms in the air, moving to the rhythmic sounds coming from nowhere and everywhere. Hips swayed in time as laughter was seen but not heard. Noise to drown out the screams.

The party just started. The party never ended. Alone in a dark room lay a corpse. An uninvited guest waiting for the beat to stop.

And the carousing went on endlessly. Everyone wondering where their host had disappeared to. A nearby bathroom. A quick shower and scrub. No one would know.

A party nearly over. Guests all but gone. Alone in a dark room lay a corpse. Screaming silently.

Food Car

#004

The aroma wafted through the train cars unabated till it reached her, beckoning. She was hungry. But she needed to stay put or risk her life to eat. Her stomach churned as the scent grew stronger.

She licked her lips.

Her hand tremors, reaching for the door. NO! She cautioned herself and turned away. She just needed to think about something else. Maybe open a window so the sweet smell had someplace to go.

Yes, that's it.

Window open, she took a deep breath. Knock on her door produced a guttural reaction she couldn't stop.

Fangs out! It's dinner time.

Bridge

#005

One hot day as old man Stone sat solemnly on his front porch he noticed someone walking across the old bridge. It startled him to his feet and before he knew it, he was running towards it.

Actually, it was more like a fast pace that would prove too much for his heart. No one was allowed to walk across the old bridge. Everyone knew that. Just like everyone knew it was Stone's responsibility to keep others away.

He clutched his chest and fell to his knees. Running was never his strong suit. Not like protecting all of humanity was.

Russian Roulette

#006

Six rounds. Four empty chambers. Three spins. Two bullets. One body slumped over a chair. Self-inflicted gun shot wound to the temple. This was more than a game of Russian Roulette but one of determination.

One bullet left. A bag of money on the table. No one knew the amount but this was never about the money. No one was here to win cash. They were here to outwit death and earn respect.

Whatever the amount, only one would be victorious and hopefully very rich. A bead of sweat fell from her brow. Gun in hand. Spin. Squeeze the trigger…

Open House

#007

They usually came in two by two, hoping to be chosen. Make a good first impression. Ask the right questions. Give the perfect answers.

In this town, houses chose their occupants. One wrong move and chances of having a place to live vanish.

In walks a young couple. Woman carrying child. Sympathy, perhaps? What house would turn down providing a home for a child?

She put the child down for a second. And there he goes. Racing down the hall, pushing open every door. Giggling all the way down a flight of stairs.

Application fine print reads: NO CHILDREN ALLOWED.

Erased
#008

She hurried down the stairs, footsteps echoed in the distance. Were they hers or was she being followed? She couldn't be sure. All she knew was that chunks of time disappeared if she closed her eyes.

That morning she was on the train. The sun was shining. Passengers around her read their newspapers. Her eyes closed, but only for a moment.

Train pulled into station waking her. Car was now empty except for one man asleep at the other end. A glance at her watch told her eight hours had ticked by.

The moon was full but her memory, erased.

Missing Ingredient

#009

The cauldron simmered as an old woman hummed her favorite tune. Preparations for her daughter's visit. They only saw each other once a year. That was the deal they made with each other when she came of age. And in return, her daughter would bring a present.

"She's here! She's here!" Squawked her macaw.

The front door opened to reveal her daughter and a man beside her.

"What are you preparing? It smells lovely," he said.

"Old family recipe. But it's missing one ingredient my daughter brought me," the old woman replied.

The man looked puzzled. They came empty handed.

The Painting

#010

He stared at the painting for what seemed like eternity. No one wondered what captivated him to the point of stillness. Security walked by a few times, but even they seemed not to notice a man sitting on a bench, staring at a painting.

It was as if he was a part of the art.

As it neared closing time he tried to look away but his eyes seemed glued to the painting. Then the figures began to move. Waving him forward. Beckoning him to join them.

His got to his feet, extended his hand and without hesitation touched life.

The Sea

#011

Sam took a long drag from her pipe and wondered what the day would bring. Having just solved a triple homicide two days ago, she was grateful for the time spent in quiet reflection on the bay in Maine. But she knew all too well that this kind of lackadaisical lifestyle would not last long. Not for her.

Sam was a woman of many talents, none of which involved resting on a lawn chair, smoking a pipe, listening to seagulls fly overhead.

Suddenly, she felt a shiver down her spine. Her phone rang. She smiled. Time to get to work.

Gumshoe

#012

I noticed her legs first through my gumshoes propped up on my desk. My admiration stopped there. She was a potential client and judging by her smeared make-up she could be a victim without my help.

Clutching a purse to her chest she sat in the chair opposite my desk, glancing over her shoulder as if being followed.

"How can I be of assistance, ma'am?" She pulled a gun from her purse. "No need for that." I raised my hands in surrender. "Someone following you?"

"She sent me." My eyes widened. How did she find me? I thought I—

BANG!

Axe

#013

I was ten when I had my first kill but it was by my two hands. Kids stuff.

Everyone in my family receives an axe on their fifteenth birthday. Today is the day for me. It's not for chopping down trees. We live in a concrete jungle, after all. No, the axe is a symbol of our birthright. A tradition passed down throughout the generations.

To be a member of this family I must use it to kill before my sixteenth birthday or suffer a fate worse than life in prison.

It's why no one can catch the Hatchet Killer.

Motherless

#014

Today is hard. Everyone has a mother. You have to or you couldn't exist. But when she doesn't exist anymore where does that leave me? Motherless? Is that a thing? It feels like a thing.

I've been motherless for…six years now (?) and it doesn't hurt any less. Everyday I get out of bed, do my chores, job my job, love my wife, care for my son, sing my favorite song when it comes on the radio. Breath in. Breath out.

Today is hard. And I know it will never be other than hard. But for some reason I'm okay.

Slay

#015

Lookin' for a pick-me-up? We'll, have we got the pill for you! With SLAY you can pill pop your troubles away. Just take one after every meal and your smile will be brighter, your appetite will be satiated, and strangers will find you irresistible.

Certain people experienced dizziness, nausea, spontaneous vomiting, bleeding eyes, and random dismemberment.

May cause sudden desire to stab your eyes out or the eyes of those around you. Don't take if you're married or may become married in the future.

Ask your doctor if SLAY is right for you. Let us make or take your day.

Fisherman

#016

Every day a small boy walked from his house in the woods to a nearby creek to catch a fish. On days where he didn't catch a fish, his family went without. On days where he caught a fish, his family praised him and thanked him for being such a great fisherman.

One day he met a man who offered to sell him a fishing rod, guaranteed to catch a fish every time. There was just one small price to pay. He could have no children.

Every day he ate fish and never went hungry till the day he died.

Mermaids

#017

"Abandon ship!"

The crew looked at each other, then back to their captain. Was he mad? Sure, the canon fire left a pretty large gaping hole in the side of their ship, but they couldn't jump now.

Lurking in the sea below were mermaids. Everyone knew what could happen if a mermaid got a hold of you. She'd never let go till she reached the ocean floor. Not the noblest of deaths.

Their captain looked to the sea, closed his eyes, and leapt into the arms of a waiting mermaid.

They watched as he disappeared deeper into the murky blue.

Split Rock

#018

Welcome to Split Rock, here to accommodate all your last life needs. Work becoming a bore? Children hassling you all day with questions you don't want to answer? Love life not as exciting as you thought it would be? At Split Rock we come equipped with bone crushing massages, soul cleansing oils, last meals, sin soaks, a full blood treatment and a movie theater too.

Beds are going fast, so act now and if you call within the next fifteen minutes we'll throw in some Quick Release after Last Meal Mints with your order.

Satisfaction Guaranteed or your life back.

Whale

#019

Maybe that dream I had as a child was true. I was a whale in my past life! Not that it mattered much now. I was chased off this cliff after all.

I don't know why this was my thought as I found myself careening towards the murky blue below. I figured the impact with the water would cushion the blow?

SPLASH!

They say you die before you even hit the water. Something about seeing your life flash before your eyes as you realize your body is going to make contact with the ocean below.

"Wow, dreams do come true!"

The Chair

#020

"Good as new, ma'am," the workman said, hoisting the chair up above his head. The old woman winced and closed her eyes, clutching her grandmother's pearls that hung around her neck.

He placed it near her fireplace. The imprint of dust still on the floorboards to mark where it lived for decades.

The comfort of her chair was paramount to her work and the workman was instructed to remain until after she sat down.

Seated, she closed her eyes, and inhaled deeply. When she opened them again a statue stood before her. Another two-timing man to add to her collection.

Mary Sue

#021

There was a young girl named Barbara Jean
Who was real smart but rather mean
She liked to make her enemies scream
There's no one quite like Barbara Jean.

Then there's the girl named Mary Sue
In her nice dress and fancy shoes
She likes to go out to parties too
That's why all the men love Mary Sue.

One night while Barbara Jean walked home
A drunk man caught her all alone.
He thought of all the evil she'd done
Not just towards him but everyone.

And just before he committed a crime
Came Mary Sue for dinner time.

Lake
#022

There were green and yellow trees just beyond the lake, as far as the eye could see, till they met with the blue sky. Frogs croaked on lily pads and fish swam happily in crystal clear water.

The first ripple was hardly noticeable. Perhaps a pebble bounced upon the water by a passerby. Then the ripple turned to waves. The happy fish were now frantic. The frogs all but vanished from sight.

Clouds rolled in from gale force winds. Shades of grey turned a bright, sunny, morning into an ominous afternoon.

A crack of lightning. THUNDER. Then came the rain.

Haunted

#023

It was just a painting. But it was also much more than a painting. The way her eyes followed all her visitors made everyone who entered that part of the exhibit move move with purpose through it. Many out of fear.

It was commissioned by a well known artist during a time when colors were far too expensive for even the noblest of men to afford. But having one's portrait captured carried with it a sense of pride, privilege, and above all, love.

Working with varying shades of grey it was as if the artist and the subject never died.

Rebuild

#024

The poster was faded and peeling at the bus stop but the key message was still visible after all this time: Help Rebuild! Karnon 2 is Here!

A super computer meant to replace Karnon 1 after the existential crisis that happened was an even bigger failure. How could humanity be expected to put its trust in a machine that once tried to eradicate them all, 'for the good of humanity.' What does a machine know about being human?

It didn't take long for the corporation behind the 1st iteration to create a sequel.

Its motto? Humanity is safer without humans.

Seasons

#025

It was meant to be a Summer house, where families gathered to remember good times. But in the Winters it remained empty. There should be no laughter from children or talk of good times from adults.

Winter was for sadness and silence. The season that always takes, leaving behind no mercy in its chilling wake. The wailing of souls but no one ever listened.

All year long they wait for a sound. A chance to be set free into the Summer sun, and inhabit the laughter from unsuspecting youth.

It is Winter still but in the distance a child laughs.

River

#026

Jazz music drowned out his beating heart as he coolly flipped his last chip in the air and let it drop in the middle of the table. Everyone gasped. Hank gulped and hoped no one noticed.

She noticed. She called.

Out came the River. This wasn't gonna be his night. That was his last chip. He owed the Boss triple already. Hank took a sip of his drink to calm his nerves.

She also took a sip from her glass. Champagne. Tall. Red lipstick left behind. Everyone waited. Even the band played softer.

Then she tossed them into the muck.

Cul-de-Sac
#027

Every house was dark but one at the end of a Cul-de-Sac. On a street where nothing ever happened.

The shadow of someone pacing could be seen from across the street.

Upon closer inspection, peering through a curtained window, half full glasses of water were evenly spread on a table in a perfect circle. A candle placed dead center.

A frantic woman paced. Stopped. Looked at them. Paced some more. Stopped. Looked again. Over and over.

Then she stopped. The glasses of water began to vibrate. The flickering flame went out. She smiled and looked towards the window.

"They're here."

Nun

#028

Every night at a quarter past five,
Twelve little nuns would take a short drive.
To a nearby bar filled with smokin' and drinkin',
And best of all, those wicked men sinnin'.

They'd save him and take him for a ride, two miles or more,
Then drop him off at the Sinner Man's door.
Where no one ever is found again.
And they thanked the Lord for good deeds, Amen!

Twelve little nuns just doing God's work,
Woke up to a house filling with smoke.
Turns out the Sinner Man wasn't done,
Till he took the wicked souls of everyone.

House for Sale

#029

House for Sale!

Looking to get your hands dirty? Build your dream house! Plenty of space for the Living (and the dead) in the backyard that can fit a party of twenty or a plot for six. Gravestones included.

The kitchen was previously used to create undisclosed meals. Three bedrooms. Cement floors throughout. No light. No windows. No closets. Use your imagination!

One open concept bathroom with a drain conveniently located in the middle. No toilet. No tub. Will throw in the hose for free!

Only accepting lowest offers!

*Any bodies found on the property are yours to keep. Honest.

Sunny Day

#030

The sun was so hot, his strut looked more like his backside was full of—well, you know. But she was a lady and so she watched, sipping her cold glass of iced tea. Waiting for his approach.

This moment was pre-arranged. Their parent's got together and decided it would be the best thing for them. He'd make his introduction, as it is always done. She'd invite him to sit with her and that would be that.

But when he sat down beside her, his odor was so pungent she wretched on his shoes. And they lived happily ever after.

News
#031

"Did you hear the news today?" She asked her husband seated at the table, newspaper covering his face.

"No, dear. That's why I'm reading the paper."

"A talking whale washed up on a beach!" He lowered his paper slowly and glared at her. She switched on the television.

Anchorwoman: This just in, it seems a whale has washed up on the coast of New Zealand and it appears to be talking. [chuckles] Bill, am I reading this right?

Anchorman: Indeed you are, Sally. And I think we have footage of its first words. Let's listen closely.

"My name is Ishmael."

Windmills

#032

She never wore matching socks. Come to think of it, she never wore matching anything. Her glasses were always on the tip of her nose as if about to reveal a secret and her hair never looked the same way twice.

She never left her apartment but she knew all there was to know about the world. Books provided both knowledge and safety. She was satisfied in her own little dream world but her friends and family were concerned.

She wished to escape into her books. Free from their accusations of madness.

She wondered what windmills were up to today.

Magic

#033

"Pick a card, any card," he said to the little girl. She nervously looked up at her mother who nodded her permission.

The girl made her selection from the fanned out deck of 52 cards and clutched it to her chest.

"Excellent. Now, think about your card. Commit it to memory. Have you got it?" The girl nodded and he pressed the deck to his forehead, eyes closed tightly in thought. "Your card is…" He opened his eyes suddenly. Shocked. "The joker? But that's impossible."

She handed the card to the confused man counting his deck over and over again.

Daughters

#034

One day, a father took his three young daughters on a picnic to tell them what they were to be when they grow up.

For his eldest, smart and quick of wit, she was to become a teacher and never marry, for her greatest love would be the children.

For his middle child, nurturing and caring, she will make a fine nurse, tending to the dying.

As for his youngest, his favorite, she will marry a man, serve him and give him one dozen children.

Therefore, after much consideration, she proceeded with her plan and handed him a poisoned sandwich.

Sacrifice

#035

Once every season the women of the village come together to discuss their husbands. Many have complaints about their lack of appreciation for all they do, and few have high praise for the love and support they receive.

While the women discuss and debate what should be done about the troublemakers, the husbands gather at the local bar to get stupid drunk in case their name comes up as the next sacrifice.

After several hours of laughter and merriment, the wives emerge with a name.

Mary's sacrifice will be rewarded with a brand new husband of her choosing next season.

The Woman

#036

What makes a world famous male detective? His quick wit? His uncanny ability to solve a mystery faster than even the most seasoned professional? No. It's the woman behind the man. The one that got away. The one that outwitted them when they were at the height of fame and notoriety.

A lesser man might scoff and pretend he was not outplayed by a woman. He may even let her get away with it.

But a greater man, admits defeat and wears it, with pride, upon his person as a reminder that once, and only once, he met his match.

Lightning
#037

Every night an old woman watched as the house next door was struck by lightning but never damaged. This happened for several nights in a row before she got the courage to pay her neighbor a visit.

As far back as she could remember, she never saw anyone leave or enter. But she always saw a man moving around inside.

A much younger man than she imagined welcomed her inside. Before she could ask her questions, lightning struck again.

She caught a glimpse of herself in a mirror and couldn't believe her eyes. A young woman stared back at her.

Swamp

#038

On the other side of a swamp lived a young woman, hiding from the wicked world her mother told her about before being consumed by the swamp.

When a strange man came upon the swamp and noticed the fair maiden seemingly talking to herself, she ran home to her hovel.

Curious to know more, he walked around the swamp and hid until she reappeared. When she finally did he stepped out and scared her so much she ran in the wrong direction.

He reached out his hand to free her from the swamp. But her mother's love got there first.

Legends
#039

Lost Dreams was a mighty pirate ship. Known for always taking treasure beyond anyone's imagination, which was how it got its name.

On its last voyage the captain, after hearing that The Isle of Legend was real from his personal chef, decided to set sail immediately. Ignoring his chef's warning that the island would not allow greedy men to find it.

The captain laughed and ordered his chef to prepare his favorite dish, whale meat soup, for all the men. That night everyone sat down to eat.

And one by one they died at the hand of The Legend Protector.

Mirrors

#040

I live in a house with no mirrors. Not because I hate the way I look. Sure, I have a self-inflicted scar on my face but it was at a moment in my life where I literally had no control. I've since learned what needs to be done.

Even my friends noticed a change within me. Even if they think the whole 'no mirrors' thing is rather strange. They have no idea why I live my life this way.

Though truthfully, I miss the sight of me!

But to see my face again could lead to the death of you.

Creation
#041

My creation is nearly complete. I've spent months perfecting it. Not letting anyone near me or it till I was good and ready. Now, after all this time I think I'm finally ready to come out of the shadows and share my creation with the world! But are they ready for it?

It's unlike anything anyone has ever seen. It had to be in order to be appreciated as much as I appreciated creating it from scratch.

Something like this only comes along once, maybe twice, in a lifetime and now my blend of coffee will go down in history!

Rumors

#042

Women walked past her, speaking in hushed tones. It turns out, Felicity may actually be innocent of her husbands death falling down a flight of stairs. If true it would be a shame. It was this rumor that earned her an invitation to this party.

She sat in the corner, shoulders squared, head held high. She wouldn't let the opinions of everyone at a party keep her from at least pretending to have a good time. After all, that's what marriage was all about.

Just ask any other widowed woman whose husband happened to fall down a flight of stairs.

Executioner

#043

Tomorrow is another Execution Day. As the executioner, I pull the lever and wait for the guilty to stop wriggling. Then I cut the rope with my axe. It's a thankless job, but one I'm good at.

As executioner I have no say in the innocence or guilt, but I decide how long they have to dangle till the crowd decides they've had enough and disperse. It's why I wear a mask. This day isn't about me. No one should remember the executioner, just the executed.

Only once did a body hold out longer than expected. And I often wondered…

Tightrope

#044

"A death defying feat! The Walking Flames will cross a tightrope, balancing batons of fire in each hand!"

The ringmaster points to the sky as two spotlights shine upon the pair.

"Without a net!" Suddenly, the net suspended below is released and pulled out of sight. The spectators are silent with anticipation. This is the act they've all been waiting for.

The pair lock eyes and take their first step. For safety they must maintain eye contact. Then someone sneezes! She looks away!

The spotlights go out. A pair of flaming batons free fall. Then a loud thud is heard.

Neighbor

#045

My new neighbor kills people. Well, not really kills them. More like she bites their neck and sucks their blood till they are reborn to live forever. How do I know? I've seen it with my own eyes!

She has no idea I even exist. And I prefer it that way. But I get hungry more than most and find myself in her kitchen, helping myself, whenever she's finished entertaining an unsuspecting soul.

I'm sure you're wondering why I don't try to help? They get eternal life!

After all, what do you expect a small mouse like me to do?

Distractions

#046

Cars stopped moving. Drivers, passengers, pedestrians on the street, all pointed towards the sky. Complete strangers asked each other what it could mean.

First it was yellow. But not sunlight yellow, this had more orange in it. Then it turned purple. Like, neon purple! Car radios interrupted their music to ask "are you seeing thing right now?"

They were all captivated. Briefly. Once the clouds reappeared and the sky returned to blue, everyone continued what they were doing as if nothing happened.

So you see, the experiment worked. If we distract the humans long enough they'd never see us coming.

Eventuality

#047

It's been 7,248 days since I left my apartment.

My alarm wakes me at 5am every morning. I get out of bed and my slippers maneuver onto my feet. I walk to my bathroom and the light turns on. Toothbrush ready. Shower starts and gets to the perfect temperature.

While I shower my clothes are already laid out on my ready made bed. I dress to the sound of classical music playing in my cochlear implants. We all have them now.

Before I begin my work day I swallow my prescribed breakfast tablets and then switch on my cortical implants.

Terminate

#048

When I'm hired to do a job I make sure it's done right, damn it. And I was hired to bring this sucker down to the grown. The Great Leveler they call me. Once I'm paid my work is all but guaranteed.

Like any good surgeon, I located the epicenter of it all. Maximum damage. Great rewards.

Five minutes. That's how much time I had to get away and still enjoy my handiwork. It wasn't till after that I saw the TERMINATE text sent two days earlier.

I said I was good at my job not at checking my messages.

Memories
#049

When my father died he left me his memory book. He claimed it could only be read by a stream where we watched the stars at night. I was just a child then but he told me one day I would understand.

Now I sit by the same stream and wait for the moon and stars just like before. But when I open the book its pages are blank! I flip through each page slowly, using the moonlight, till I find a message on the last page:

If you remember us the words will come like stars in the sky.

The Rabbit
#050

A rabbit spoke to me today. I know how it sounds. But this wasn't your ordinary rabbit. He wore a waist coat, expensive dress shoes, a bowler hat, and spectacles. I've always felt compelled to trust anyone who wore glasses. I realize he's a rabbit! No need to keep reminding me.

He assured me the reason for his appearance was a matter of life or death, not just for me, but all of humanity. Turns out a great evil is plotting their return to our world, bringing destruction and bad breath in its wake.

And I really hate bad breath!

LeRoy

#051

"Give me five to win on Sundance Kid," LeRoy said, grabbed his ticket and sat in a chair nearest the speaker.

"And they're off…"

He tried to listen to the announcer speed through the race but was distracted by an old man seated beside him. Eyes closed, he seemed to be repeating the same words under his breath. LeRoy leaned in closer and heard, "Sundance Kid to win."

The race ended but LeRoy had no idea who won. Annoyed men walked by while others held their tickets tightly to collect their winnings.

"Not to worry LeRoy, I'm sure you won."

Ferryman

#052

These days it's easy to get to the other side. A simple boat ride and you're there. As a child I was told it's paradise. Like an endless picnic of good food, music, and people to talk to (or ignore) depending on my mood. I wonder if that's true?

I've been on this boat for what seems like eternity. No one to talk to but an old ferryman. I ask him if we're there yet. Surely, he must have other passengers waiting to make the same journey as I am?

His response is always the same, "Your time will come."

Knight

#053

A snake hissed and slithered on a tree branch near a window of the castle. It listened as a rather short and stout knight was awarded a sword for bravery and valor in the face of danger.

Continuing to hiss in disagreement, the snake dropped down to the floor unnoticed and slithered its way towards the knight.

The snake would show them all that bravery and valor meant nothing against poisonous venom. Instant death.

Down by the knight's ankles it opened its mouth about to bite down when the knight placed the sword down beside him, through the snake's head.

Again

#054

Every morning I wake up in another person's body. It started happening after my thirteenth birthday. I never know who. I never know where. I've tried to stay awake but that doesn't work.

I was born twice and died five times. Oh, and I even murdered someone once with a really big kitchen knife.

I'm fuzzy about my age, my gender, or what I'm supposed to look like at this point. I don't have any friends, so I don't have enemies. They say getting a second chance to do it all over again is a blessing. What about a million?

Starless Sky
#055

Her feet dangled over the edge of the roof her seven story apartment building. Bare feet. Painted black toe nails. She turned on her teal Studebaker AM/FM radio, tuned to her favorite station.

"This song goes out to all the wild women flying in that starless sky. You know who you are."

It was like her favorite broadcaster knew exactly what she wanted to hear. He spoke directly to her soul. It was a sign. The one she waited for her whole life. The lyrics buzzed through her body. She swayed side to side, closed her eyes and leapt.

Stolen

#056

"Welcome to another hour of macabre musical tracks! Somewhere out there I hope there's a Johanna just waiting to be stolen."

The truck hit a bump along an old gravel road. Headlights off so not to arouse suspicion. Radio loud enough for the driver and his passenger to hear. He hummed along to the song, tapping the wheel hypnotically.

Moonlight broke through the sycamore trees revealing a dilapidated Victorian house, long abandoned by time and money.

He lowered the cab of his truck and pulled her bound legs towards him. Hoisting her over one shoulder her name tag falls. JOHANNA.

Stop

#057

Her gas tank was just over three quarters empty and a sign up ahead said she wouldn't see another gas station or rest stop for sixty miles. She pulled off at the next exit, excited at the prospect of stretching her legs.

Engine switched off, she opened her door and winced from the loud gas station music.

"…on hot Summer days I just want a beer, a drag, and a Fancy tune. How 'bout we light it up…"

She pulled a cigarette and match from her pocket, then releasing the nozzle from its cradle, stood still, letting gasoline drip out.

Heartless

#058

Waiting at a drive thru her favorite song came on the radio so she turned it up. When it got to her favorite part she belted the words like no one was watching. "What'll it be?"

She shouted her order, refusing to turn it down till it finished, and pulled up to the next window to get her food.

"That one goes out to all the heart broken girls secretly wishing to be heartless."

Bag on her lap she pulled away. While at a stop light she reached in for her burger and pulled out her still beating heart instead.

Lie in Wait

#059

"If you've got a best friend named Jolene, be warned. I hear she's a man snatcher."

Heather lit a cigarette and lowered the volume on the station playing in her ears. She leaned against a tree and waited. No one paid her any attention while she watched her ex-boyfriend who was also waiting. For her.

When he waved to someone in the distance, a tear rolled down Heather's cheek. Her cigarette fell and she snuffed it as she walked towards them.

"…and I cannot compete with you…"

"JOLENE!" A gunshot left her auburn hair mixed with blood on the ground.

Buried

#060

"What a weird song to play at a bowling alley, amiright?"

My friend and I giggled sneakily at the guy behind the shoe counter who looked just like a member of the Beatles.

"And just like that, poor Eleanor is no more. You've been listening to…" We laughed louder realizing it was a radio station playing and not a CD.

"Ellie, you're up," I said, then the power went out! I heard screams around me. "Ellie?" I whispered in a panic.

Lights came back on and there she was at the end of the lane, buried under hundreds of pins.

The End

#061

She kissed him sweetly before he got in his truck and drove away. She walked to her bathroom and turned on a light.

"I knew a Delilah once, and she deserved to have the grin wiped from her face too. If you feel the same, this one's for you."

He got out his car, leaving the door wide open, the song blasting into the night sky. He crossed the road to her front door and rang her doorbell.

Her laughter came before she opened the door then faded when she saw him standing there with a knife blocking the moonlight.

Gary

#062

"Man, this is crazy. Are you sure that machine of yours is right?" I dug my shovel into the ground as far as it would go.

"Dude, I'm telling you, this thing detects gold. Just dig. Trust me. Gary doesn't lie."

"Gary? Who the f—." I stopped short when my shovel made contact with something. "What was that?" I looked at Jim (whose name isn't Gary) and we both dropped to our knees and started digging with our hands.

"Oh, hell naw!" Staring up at me was a skull with one gold tooth. "Looks like Gary found more than gold."

Scalpel
#063

"Let's see who we have with us this evening," Shirley said, pulling up a photograph of the dead woman laying on her table. She read her statistics off the computer to an empty room. "Mrs. Katherine Chambers. Forty-eight. Stroke. No children. Damn."

She started her favorite playlist of classical music and held up her best scalpel, ready to begin.

"I wish you could speak. I would ask about your life. What went wrong. What went right."

"I'm sure that's none of your business." The scalpel slipped and landed in Katherine's open mouth.

"Who said that?" She eyed the corpse suspiciously.

Lighthouse

#064

I'm a lighthouse keeper but I don't help ships at sea. My job is to keep an eye on the skies. We know it will come again as it always does. And so I wait. I've been waiting for over five years now.

Till one night, during a rain storm, the sky lit up. I thought it was lightning and ignored it but the thud that followed was unmistakable. I'd heard it before. The aerial was back.

During every visit it takes two humans, "for learning purposes" it says. Then it returns them the same way, dropped from the sky.

Dirt

#065

Dirt. Hardened over time. No flowers needed to mark the spot. It's committed to our memories forever. Under the tree where I once carved our names. And now, here you are, working up a sweat (again), digging a space to fill with more memories.

Photographs and trinkets that remind you of us. Wasted time covering them in the same dirt you haven't dared visit in over a decade. I can't help but wonder, why now? What's changed? Do you feel the guilt of leaving me alone all this time or have you moved on?

After all, you buried me here.

White Lace

#066

A "Just Married" sign on the back of the new Camaro began to fade from the sun and endless driving. Almost empty, the driver had to stop at the nearest gas station. He leaned over and kissed the bride on her tear stained cheeks, then cranked her window open for air. Her veil caught in the wind.

"How 'bout our favorite song while you wait?" The Carpenters startled the station attendant who smiled and waved at the couple suspiciously.

Back on the road the driver smiled at her through the rearview mirror, her smeared lipstick matching her blood-soaked wedding dress.

Henry

#067

I spend most days and nights at a local pub. Everyone knows me and those who don't, wind up talking to me one way or another before they leave. Usually it's because of my friend Henry. He's known to stand out in a crowd because of what he is.

See, Henry is my imaginary friend. He showed up the day I killed my wife. I realize it's a bit unorthodox to have an imaginary friend at my age. And you probably want to hear about my murdered wife. Unfortunately for you, my friend Henry thinks I should have another drink.

Afterlife

#068

"Welcome, Mr. and Mrs. Smith, to Heavenly Meadows. Open day and night to serve your afterlife needs."

:groan:

How droll. The computer helps the living decide what they want. I deal with the dead. They talk less and ultimately end up with whatever I give them.

Take this couple as an example. Innocently planning to make their afterlife arrangements easier and more efficient for loved ones and friends. HA!

I wear black so I can lurk in dark corners of the room where they can't see me smiling as they give us all their money and I give 'em hell!

Hitchhicker

#069

"Where you headed?" Davey asks our passenger like he's genuinely interested in the answer.

"No place in particular. Just out of this God forsaken town, that's for sure." They both laugh. Davey likes to pretend he understands their struggles. I roll my eyes and turn up the radio. I'm driving so it's ladies choice and I prefer talk radio.

"Bonnie & Clyde have struck again! Police say they murdered another unidentifiable hitchhiker. This is their third victim in a week…"

I lock eyes with Davey. An undeniable connection passes silently between us. Then I look in the rearview mirror. He knows.

Sight

#070

When I was a child, my father and I fought all the time. Especially, after the surgery. I didn't want it. And I hated him for doing it to me. Then he died shortly after and now I spend the rest of my life wishing I could thank him.

As a scientist for the new world government he knew what was coming, and as his son I would be a perfect candidate for testing. But when they saw I had no eyes, I became the only human without government implants. They call me Mr. Johnson, the only living free man.

Breakfast

#071

Every morning I stand in the kitchen and prepare breakfast for my husband before he leaves for work. Two strips of bacon. Two sunny side up eggs. White toast. Lightly buttered. And black coffee.

By the time the toaster dings I hear him pull the chair out at the kitchen table and sit with the morning paper unfolded, reading aloud to himself. I place his plate down carefully in front of him and hold my breath. Waiting.

He glances at the plate and smiles. I breathe and sit across from him. The chain around my ankle rattles in the silence.

Fog
#072

It was a simple barbecue. A welcome back party for the newlyweds. He was all smiles. She was positively radiant.

We all came together, to celebrate, again. We drank sub-par wine, though I noticed the bride only drank water, and reminisced. No one mentioned the possible fog forecast. It would've been in poor taste to mention the creepers. And upon reflection I'm thankful for two things:

One, that my bladder could never hold liquor for long. And two, that the creepers devoured the party while I was peeing. It got me out of having to admit how bored I was.

Kiss

#073

Maybe it was the lack of a case that made me vulnerable to whoever entered my office. Or maybe it was the way her red lipstick matched her auburn hair peeking through her black head scarf.

She didn't say much. Women like her never do. They let their eyes do the talking. And her eyes told me she was in trouble. I didn't think I was the man for her till she kissed me into submission.

I didn't catch her name, just that her life was in danger and I had to kill him.

It was a damn good kiss…

Lady Liv

#074

"Gentlemen, if I can draw your attention to the stage. The show you've all been waiting for is about to begin."

Heavy purple curtains part down the middle and a spotlight comes on from above to illuminate Lady Liv for her one and only performance of the night. She smiles and the men are captivated. Frozen in time and space as she sings just for them.

Suddenly, black hooded figures work their way through the tables, unnoticed, lifting wallets and jewelry. Leaving empty pockets and souls in their wake.

Lady Liv stops singing. The spot light goes out. Curtains close.

Pie
#075

According to Harry, the owner of the Salty Shack in the sleazy side of town, my wife's been meeting her lover here multiple times a week. "Another late night at the office, dear." Her cold texts. What a fool I've been!

We have an arrangement, Harry and I. Whenever they arrive he calls me and I watch them from across the street. Ten times he's called and ten time I've done nothing about it. But tonight will be different.

Tonight I'm going to join them and let them squirm as I eat their pie with a grin on my face.

Vinny

#076

"Vinny here?" The bar teemed with customers. Some new. Some old. All with a past and a story. The bartender nodded towards the other end of the main floor. Our unlucky man, Mr. James Horner, owes Vinny, my boss, some money. And when you owe Vinny money, you want to make sure you pay him, or else.

Horner ordered his usual drink and knocked it back before squaring his shoulders and weaving through the throng of tables. I could tell by his gait that his pockets were empty.

Me? I much rather listen to the lovely lady singing on stage.

Lola

#077

I work all hours, unlike my boss, Vinny. I have to, what with the club always open. Take the mornin' crowd, for instance. Some just want their coffee and a little entertainment. So, we provide the best that money can't buy.

I prefer the mornin's because it's when Lola comes in to ask if there's any news. See, her beau gambled away their life savings, even borrowed some from the house, that's when his luck ran out. Five years later and she's still lookin' for him here.

Vinny stopped lookin' years ago. I just haven't the heart to tell her.

Brat

#078

"Ladies and gentlemen, the Nouveau is proud to present, Ms. L—"

"Watch out, here comes a Darkie," a man formerly known as Brat (because he always orders bratwurst whenever he comes to the club), decides to whisper under his breath. Except, it was loud enough for everyone to hear.

I glanced over at Vinny who nodded to a couple of gentlemen he employs to deal with men like Brat, who, before he could protest his innocence was gone. Leaving behind the muffled cries of a forgotten man.

The lights went down, one spotlight, as a heavenly voice began to sing.

Harper

#079

I wish I could dance. But I've got two left feet. Ever since I was born my momma always said I would be a better musician than a singer or dancer. My momma was always right and a great judge of character. It's a gift she passed on to me.

For instance, I could tell by the way Hank wasn't tending bar that his sister, Harper, was expected at any moment. She knew just how to push his buttons. Asking for money or alcohol.

Then, she walked in on the arm of some man and immediately hit the dance floor.

Donna & Sheryl

#080

"Dinner at five. Evening news at six while reading the paper till sunset, then straight to bed," Donna Jones said. Two ladies sit huddled together, nursing drinks so long the ice melted.

"No…" Sheryl Tiegs, her best friend of fourteen years, makes the universal sign with her hand for 'you know…' and Donna shakes her head.

"Never on a weeknight."

"Same!" They both giggle and clink glasses.

"I'll sneak out to your place and leave the backdoor open. Kitchen knife on the counter for you."

"Same!" They snort simultaneously. The best laid plans decided over drinks happen every day here.

Cass
#081

"She's checking you out, Billy. You should ask for her number." A couple of boys coming of age. My guess? It's Billy's birthday and his so called friends are ready to make him a man.

Billy shakes his head. Smart kid. His friends? Not so much. One of them gets Cass's attention then he reaches over to pinch her bottom before she can back away.

She grabs his drink and throws it in his face.

"Trouble, Cass?" I ask as she places her tray on my piano.

"Nothin' you can't handle, suga," she answers with a smile and a wink.

Sam

#082

"Sam here? Send him my way would ya." Pin stripe suit. Clean shaven. Walkin' money. "And a martini."

There's only one Sam I know and she ain't no fella. I had a feelin' Mr. Pin Stripe would be in for a surprise.

She came up behind me and with her hands over my eyes whispered in my ear, "guess who?" She smelled of bourbon and peaches. Two of my favorite things.

"Watch out with that one, Sam. He thinks you're a fella."

"I wish!" She walked away, and I admired the way she wore a man's suit better than me.

Momma

#083

I was a panhandler. Scraping just enough to pay a quarter to Reems, the owner of a halfway house at the stockyards. It was more of a shack than a house but that's not the point of this 'ere story.

All I owned at the time, besides the clothes on my back, was a baby piano my momma scraped together and gifted me on my fifteenth birthday before she sent me into the world to fend for myself.

Vinny heard me playin' one night and I was hired on the spot. I've lived at The Nouveau Revue Nightclub ever since.

Ingrid

#084

"...I can do card tricks..." She answered, though rather timidly. The act we had just seen was really quite impressive and she knew it.

On Tuesday afternoons we hold auditions to find new talent. But shaky Ingrid seemed to be out of her element. That is, until she was bold enough to perform her card trick on Vinny.

Many women and men have crumpled just being near him. But not Ingrid. She was determined to impress us all.

And like me, he realized her true talent was wasted being a magician when she could earn twice as much catching thieves.

Drew

#085

We love whenever military men come round for a visit. They eat and drink for free. But what we don't see often are women dressed in uniform. So, when three walk in, everyone notices. Present company included.

"Ladies, any requests? My fingers are itchin' to play somethin' just for ya." I couldn't quite place the colors but blood red seemed an odd choice.

"We're just dying to sink our teeth into some fellas. Play whatever will bring them our way." Lieutenant Drew winked at me and I smiled back cautiously.

There are some branches of the military I don't question.

Fats

#086

"I'm a salesman, not a miracle worker. Even I can't make you thinner," Gerald said. He was joined by a man so large his chair disappeared beneath his massive backside.

"Name your price. I'm good for it," Fats said, a platter of cannoli's placed in front of him.

"Well," Gerald said, "I do have this one thing." He placed a bottle of clear liquid on the table. "But I don't recommend it."

A stack of hundreds was dropped on the table and the bottle emptied without another word. Suddenly, Fats clutched his throat.

"Glue," Gerald said. "Works almost every time."

Herb & Cyn

#087

They wore matching dark cheaters, black berets, black pants, and long sleeve shirts, black, in the Summer time. After dark. I stifled a chuckle as they approached the bar and ordered two mint juleps brought to their table.

She carried their drinks while he led the way towards an empty table. Posers from a long forgotten era.

"Shall we stay a while, Herb?" she asked, swaying her hips to the music.

"I dig the vibe, Cyn. I ain't never felt more alive." Cyn started to sit but Herb pulled the chair out too far and she fell.

Two wasted juleps.

Lace

#088

"AAAAHHHHH!!!" I heard the screams and nodded to the conductor to play something louder.

At the start of our nightshift, Lace, one of our girls, came in with a shiner no make-up could hide. She knew it needed to be reported to Vinny. If there's one thing he hates, it's a man who raises his hands to a woman.

The door to his private office opened briefly and I could see a mound on the floor. Half alive. Half rat begging for mercy.

Lace entered his office for the best part. When the song finished there were no more screams.

The Dancers

#089

One night a week I watch a couple walk onto the dance floor. Both tall and thin. He spins her mercilessly. Her movements match his precisely as they sway to music that isn't playing.

She twirls across the floor and he quickly glides after. Brings her close and together they are melody in motion. She wants to resist. End the dance. Walk away. I see it in her face. The way her body leans slightly away.

Then they stop suddenly. The nightclub is closed. Nobody but me and my piano.

He reaches out and she places her hand in his.

Mr. Horner
#090

Mr. Horner returns, looking a lot different than he did last time I saw him. Clean shaven. New suit and lady on his arm.

She's the kind any man would be proud to have on his arm till she opens her mouth and reveals her beauty only goes so far.

He flashes a wad of bills to enter the back room where only the high rollers are allowed.

On Vinny's orders, I steer clear. A room like that can strip a man of more than his wallet. And Mr. Horner's about to discover in that room the devil always wins.

Jake

#091

"Hey you, boy," she said. "Where is he? My Jake says he was barred from ever returning."

I remember her son. Tall and lanky. Total opposite of his mother. Came in last night and got handsy with one of our waitresses. He's lucky that's all that happened.

"I don't think so," I said and returned to playing my piano. "But I'll tell him you stopped by."

"I know who you are. No one's ever seen you leave this place. Slave or friend, I wonder?" I want to wipe the smile off her face, if only I could follow after her.

Melody

#092

There's a story of young lovers. It's the same story wherever you go. He loves her. She can't love him. In every instance the constant is always the melody. The music that plays out around them.

The laughter. The tears. The memories.

I represent a man who once sat at a piano not unlike mine and witnessed tragedy, hate, and love. He told me that I was not to influence their story, just sing it.

As long as I have my piano, I don't need a story of my own. I live on through the songs I sing about you.

Falling Star

#093

In a bedroom is a boy who should be asleep. Instead, he sits at his large open window, staring up at the moon, wishing he could fly. If only he could just reach out his hand and touch it. He would race the shooting stars and finally be free.

A loud snore from the bedroom next door startles him and he falls out! His fingers clutch the ledge.

Suddenly, he sees a star fall from the sky and hover over his head. "Let go, Peter."

He opens his hand. The rush of air and a star follows his fast descent.

Crocodile & Snake

#094

"Eww! What a ssssmelly exisssstence it must be for you to live in ssssuch ssssqualor," the snake hissed down at a very hungry crocodile. "Not much of a talker, I ssssee."

The snake slithered down till it was eye-level with the crocodile and noticed its eyes were closed. "Hmm, ssssleeping I ssssee. Typical of sssswamp animalssss."

A tree branch snapped in the distance, making the snake's eyes dart in its general direction. More of its long body uncoiling. Then snap!

The crocodile lowered its head back into the swamp, waiting for the next smart snake to pay it a visit.

Sheet Music

#095

It was heartbreaking news. There was only one thing for her to do. She walked over to her record player, pulled the needle head up and to the right to start it, then dropped.

The familiar crackle before the music started calmed her instantly. A recording of her mother playing the violin. It was a memory so strong she could see her standing in the middle of the living room, three pages of handwritten sheet music on the stand, through her childhood and teen years. But noticeably absent for her wedding and divorce. And now she would join her soon.

Feathers of Four

#096

"You must let me go, father. I am the only one who can save us, it is prophecy," said Maylin, the elf daughter of King Goren. She speaks of a prophecy bestowed upon her at birth.

"Hang the damn prophecy. You are my heir and my daughter. Were your mother still alive…" his voice cracked at the memory of his wife.

Maylin placed her hands upon his, "She would not stand in the way of prophecy. She would want me to find the Feathers of Four to save us."

King Goren nodded in agreement. The child he knew was gone.

Petunias

#097

My story starts on Main Street. Where lost souls go to be forgotten and dead bodies are disposed of regularly. It's where I examined her fifth victim. Trussed up on a chair in the middle of the road. He'd been there for days before someone called it in due to the unbearable stench.

That's my job. Duty bound to catch her before she kills someone really important. This one's an upgrade from her last four victims. Nice watch. Expensive suit.

In his lapel, one flower. I'm allergic to flowers. But to confirm it's her I take a sniff. Petunias.

ACHOO!

Elevator

#098

"Going down." I handed the elevator operator a piece of paper. He didn't bother opening it. He'd seen the familiar red color before. He knew what it meant. I tried to catch his eye and smile for reassurance that everything was going to be okay but he avoided eye contact as he guided the doors closed, and pushed the button for the sixth floor.

It began a slow descent then lurched to a stop suddenly, and the heart I no longer had, sank. I'd only heard rumors about the sixth floor but no one dared to speculate further.

Doors opened.

Invited Guests

#099

The host was late, but his guests were too busy enjoying the fabulous spread of food to notice or care. Pretty soon everyone wondered how they came to be invited.

No one was willing to admit their friendships were fake. They didn't like the host but it was a secret they would take to their grave. Better to be kind and alive than truthful and dead.

When the host finally arrived, he seemed preoccupied, uneasy. He knew the dangers of inviting all of his frenemies.

Then eight people sat down to dine. Everything was going great till the host died.

Dragons

#100

"I'm telling you, it's real. I saw it with my own eyes." Everyone at the Bar on 8th broke out in laughter. No one ever believed Tommy "Sink" Jones. They called him that because drinking was like pouring liquor down a drain. No one knew how he could drink so much.

"Hey, Sink, I bet it was so tall it could touch the moon?" shouted a voice in the crowd.

"Nice try, Herb. It's in the caves I'm tellin' ya. Sleepin' like a baby."

Patrons murmured that he was drunk and went about their conversations, unfazed.

"Here there be dragons!"

"A short story must have a single mood and every sentence must build towards it."

— Edgar Allan Poe

to be continued...

themes index

Themes are how I come up with the ideas for the stories you've just read. I hope knowing this information will help you better understand why I wrote each one and you'll go back to reread and see how they are uniquely connected.

Story #032 - #053
Major Arcana (Literary Tarot) | Pages 72 - 115

Brink Literacy Project, is a nonprofit organization dedicated to changing the world through storytelling. The Literary Tarot, brings together some of the greatest authors and cartoonists of our time to pair a tarot card with a seminal book that embodies the meaning of the arcana.

When I first heard of this deck I knew two things right away:

1. I wanted to own this amazing deck.
2. They would be amazing inspiration for at least 78 new stories for my 100 word stories journey.

Story #055 - #075
Song Lyrics | Pages 118 - 159

They say a song can elicit emotions long after you've heard it for the first time. Feelings of deja vu and memories from years ago. Each of these songs made me feel something deep down in my soul.

I recommend listening to each song and then return to its companion story to get a deeper understanding of what I was trying to say.

Story #076 - #092
Classic Songs from Musicals | Pages 160 - 193

Musicals remind me of my childhood. They take me back to sitting on the hardwood floor in my living room when I was really young, watching Fred Astaire, Judy Garland, Lena Horne, and others. My mom introduced me to musicals.

A series of stories that all happen in the same place but not necessarily the same time; Club Nouveau. Each story features a different person who's been in the club for one reason or another.

Vinny | Get Happy from Summer Stock (1950), pg. 160
performed by Judy Garland

Lola | Good Morning from Singin' in the Rain (1952), pg. 162
performed by Gene Kelly, Debbie Reynolds, and Donald O'Connor

Brat | Paper Doll from Two Girls and a Sailor (1942), pg. 164
performed by Lena Horne

Harper | My Baby Loves Me from Viva Las Vegas (1964), pg. 166
performed by Ann Margaret and Elvis Presley

Donna & Sheryl | Bosom Buddies from Mame (1974), pg. 168
performed by Lucille Ball and Bea Arthur

Cass | What a Swell Party This is from High Society (1956), pg. 170
performed by Frank Sinatra and Bing Crosby

Sam | I Don't Care from In the Good Old Summertime (1949), pg. 172
performed by Judy Garland

Momma | Ol' Man River from Showboat (1936), pg. 174
performed by Paul Robeson

Ingrid | Take Back Your Mink from Guys and Dolls (1955), pg. 176
performed by Vivian Blaine

Drew | What Good is a Gal Without a Guy from Skirts Ahoy! (1952), pg. 178
performed by Joan Evans, Vivian Blaine, and Esther Williams

Fats | Ya Got Trouble from The Music Man (1962), pg. 180
performed by Robert Preston

Herb & Cyn | Clap Yo Hands from Funny Face (1957), pg. 182
performed by Fred Astaire and Kay Thompson

Lace | Beat Out Dat Rhythm on a Drum from Carmen Jones (1957), pg. 184
performed by Pearl Bailey

The Dancers | Let's Face the Music and Dance from Follow the Fleet (1936), pg. 186
performed by Fred Astaire and Ginger Rogers

Mr. Horner | Taking a Chance on Love from Cabin in the Sky (1943), pg. 188
performed by Ethel Waters

Jake | Moon River from Breakfast at Tiffany's 1957), pg. 190
performed by Audrey Hepburn

Melody | As Time Goes By from Casablanca (1942), pg. 192
performed by Dooley Wilson

Story #093 - #100
Ink Suit (Literary Tarot) | Pages 194 - 209

The Second 100

Thank you for reading my first book of 100 word stories. It was truly a labour of love and a true passion project of mine to get to this point. If you enjoyed them, and are hungry for even more stories you can read in one sitting, then let your next purchase be The Second 100.

In this collection I bring more story continuity with common threads for you to discover. There's also the very first of its kind, Pentober. An idea that combines storytelling with the age old tradition of writing a story by hand, using pen and paper.

acknowledgements

First, to my fellow writers who've joined me in writing 100 word stories through collaboration. And those of you on your own 100 word writing journeys alongside me.

To my newsletter subscribers for reading my daily 100 word stories and in doing so declaring me the Queen of 100 Word Stories. If not for your commitment to reading them I'd never have published this collection.

And lastly, to my paid subscribers. You let me know you believe in my work through your contributions and for that I am honored:

Ben M.

Edward R.

Brennan Q.

Natalie P.

Diana

Kim H.

about me

Erica L. Drayton was born in the Bronx, in NYC. She began writing stories almost immediately after she learned how to read and write from her mother, a former English teacher. As a gay, black, woman, Erica used storytelling as a way to express her feelings through poetry and fantasy novels at a young age.

After college, she took her continued passion for storytelling and developed it further, into writing short stories, eventually challenging herself to write 100 word stories.

She lives with her wife, young son, two dogs, and eight chickens in the Capital Region of Upstate New York.

erica drayton writes

Erica Drayton Writes is a newsletter that sends daily 100 Word Stories as well as updates on her countless other writing projects. She doesn't just write 100 word stories every single day. If that weren't enough, she also does all she can to inspire others to write 100 word stories on a regular basis.

If you subscribe today, you will receive a story every day that will make you think and one day give you the bug to try your own storytelling.

You can also upgrade for access to her comprehensive archive of 100 word stories, serials, and much more.

Milton Keynes UK
Ingram Content Group UK Ltd.
UKHW051843290324
440093UK00004B/12